No secret stays hidden forever.
A HIDDEN FIRE
Elemental Mysteries Book One

❧❦❧

A phone call from an old friend sets Dr. Giovanni Vecchio back on the path of a mysterious manuscript he's hunted for over five hundred years. He never expected a young student librarian could be the key to unlock its secrets, nor could he have predicted the danger she would attract.

Now he and Beatrice De Novo follow a twisted maze that leads from the archives of a university library, though the fires of Renaissance Florence, and toward a confrontation hundreds of years in the making.

History and the paranormal collide in A Hidden Fire, the first book in the bestselling Elemental Mysteries series and semifinalist in the Kindle Book Review's Best Indie Books of 2012.

A Hidden Fire is a paranormal mystery/romance for adult readers. It is the first book in the Elemental Mysteries Series.

THE ELEMENTAL MYSTERIES
A Hidden Fire
This Same Earth
The Force of Wind
A Fall of Water

A HIDDEN FIRE

Elemental Mysteries Book One

ELIZABETH HUNTER